ROBROY
LIBRARY

No 16

1d

THE MYSTERY OF THE LONELY CAIRN

"Diarmid's face wore an awed look as he gazed at the strange drawings on the cairn. 'This is not canny, Chief,' he said, 'there is a meaning in all this, and I think the fairies have done it.'"

POCKET BUDGET LIBRARY

NOW ON SALE.

GRAND COMPLETE STORIES

IN ATTRACTIVE ILLUSTRATED COLOURED COVERS.

1. SONS OF THE WAVES. A Stirring Story of Fighting at Sea.
2. JACK MARLIN'S SCHOOLDAYS. A Story of Rattling Fun and Adventures at School.
3. WITH THE FUSILIERS; Or, Brothers in Arms. An Exciting Soldier Story.
4. BELTRANO THE NAMELESS; Or, The Cavaliers of Castile. A Grand Old-Time Tale of the Days of Chivalry.
5. THE PIKEMEN OF SEDGEMOOR. The Story of the Daring Adventures of Dick Seymour.
6. MIDSHIPMAN JACK MARLIN. A Splendid Story of Adventure at Sea.
7. IN THE RANKS. A Rattling Story of Adventure in India.
8. ULLAM THE UNKNOWN. A Stirring Story of the Scottish Wars.
9. LOYAL TO THE KING. A Grand Story of Remarkable Adventure.
10. DICK ASHTON OF CRANWORTH. A Rattling School Story.
11. ON THE SPANISH MAIN. Jack Marlin's Further Adventures at Sea
12. SWORD AND CROSSBOW; Or, The Rightful Heir of Battleden.
13. WHO SERVES THE KING? A Stirring Story of Adventure in the Days of King Charles.
14. THE GRAMMAR SCHOOL BRIGADE; Or, The Rattling Adventures of Eight Schoolboys.
15. AFLOAT AND ASHORE. The Further Exciting Adventures of Lieutenant Jack Marlin.
16. THE GOLDEN KNIGHT; Or, The Secret of the Crown of Iona.
17. THE BOYS OF REDMINSTER. A School Story full of Fun and Adventures.
18. CAPTAIN JACK MARLIN. His Adventures in the Four Quarters of the Globe.
19. RUPERT, THE YOUNG SWORDSMAN. A Grand Old-Time Story.
20. FIGHTING JACK. A Thrilling Soldier Story.
21. THE SCHOOLBOY DETECTIVE. A Sequel to "The Boys of Redminster." A Grand School Tale.
22. THE LOST GALLEON. A Thrilling Story of Adventure in Search of Hidden Treasure.
23. THE DASHING DRAGOON. A Stirring War Story.
24. THE KNIGHT OF THE SILVER CROSS. A Most Exciting Old-Time Story.
25. THE MYSTERY OF FARNLEIGH COLLEGE. A Splendid School Story.
26. SAVED FROM THE SEA. A Rattling Sea Story of Stirring Adventure.
27. IN THE VAN OF BATTLE. A Grand Story of Fighting.
28. FENELON THE FEARLESS. An Old-Time Story full of Daring Deeds.

EACH BOOK CONTAINS A LONG COMPLETE STORY OF ABOUT 38,000 WORDS.

Each Number Price ONE PENNY; by Post, 1½d.

London: JAMES HENDERSON & SONS, Red Lion House, Red Lion Court, Fleet Street, E.C.

THE MYSTERY OF THE LONELY CAIRN

By ERSKINE BLAIR.

CHAPTER I.

THE HATCHING OF A PLOT.

" THE red thief shall die ! "

" Ay, by the rood, I've a silver bullet in my pouch that cannot miss its mark, and I'm keeping it for Rob Roy Mac-Gregor. What say you, Geordie ? Are you not of like mind with us ? "

" I am that. He has put scorn upon me more than once, but saying is easier than doing. You may meet him with the sword, but so surely as you do so you'll never handle the haft of your clay-more again. A silver bullet cannot miss its mark, they say. But when you hide in the heather or behind the wall, it may be, and cock your firelock, there'll be another man behind you cocking his firelock, and he'll be a MacGregor, and what's more, he'll fire before you have time to crook your finger, and his mark will be your head. Rob Roy goes well guarded. To take a fox you must trap him."

" What would ye do then, Geordie ? "

" I have my own plans. If your bullet misses, I'll trap the fox. But whatever is done must be done in secret, and with no witnesses by, or it may come to the ears of the MacGregors."

Three men were gathered about the fireplace in a smoky buddel, or drinking shop—three enemies to the chief of the MacGregors, three determined ruffians.

The first was John Grahame, a large, fair man, with cold, glittering eyes of steely blue. He was a powerful, quarrel-some fellow, ever ready to draw his claymore upon the smallest affront.

The second man, he who boasted of the silver bullet, was a Campbell, but was held in no great favour by the head of his clan, the Duke of Argyll, who was, upon the whole, favourably dis-posed towards Rob Roy.

George Murray, who had advocated craft rather than force as a means for the discomfiture of Rob Roy, was the most dangerous man of the three. A sour-looking, dark fellow, with a scar across his nose which did not add to the attractiveness of his countenance ; he had long hated Rob Roy, and a recent raid of the MacGregors, in which some of the Murray's cattle had been driven off, had not tended to lessen his ill-feeling against the chief of that wild clan.

" Let us empty another flask of aquavitæ to the success of our plans," suggested Campbell. " Ho, there, Davy ; another pint of liquor ! "

A strange, unkempt lad came in to attend to the wants of these three visitors to the lonely wayside inn. Davy—Daft Davy, as he was commonly called—did most of the work of the house, his master being too fond of the taste of his own wares to be able to attend much to business on six days out of seven. It was only upon the Sabbath that the innkeeper could be said to be strictly sober.

Davy, with his weak smile and wander-ing eye, hovered about the three men, as they drank, and told one another again and again that Rob Roy must die. They knew where the chief was in hiding. He was dwelling with his kinsman, Diarmid, for the present, in Diarmid's lonely farmhouse. It would not be wise to attack him there; his clansmen might come to hear of it. But when he chose to leave his lair he must go by one of three ways. The house stood in a narrow valley at the foot of a precipitous cliff, and, on leaving it, the chief must either go up the valley or down the valley or over the hill opposite the house.

Grahame would watch one end of the valley, Campbell the other, and Murray would be on the watch in case Rob Roy should take to the hills. These details being settled, not without much noise and wrangling, the three valiant topers got drunk and finally fell asleep.

In the chilly dawn, when the fire was out, they awoke, one after the other, each going out into the bleak morning air as he woke, without a word to his companions; and each as he went his way pondered over what he had said on the previous evening, when full of pot-valour; each regretted having pledged his word to engage in a risky enterprise, but none of them dared, for fear of incurring the scorn of the others, to draw back from the plot they had hatched against their common enemy.

CHAPTER II.

The Red Arrows.

" I would have you bide here longer yet, Rob Roy," said Diarmid MacGregor to his great kinsman, when the chief, one evening, announced his attention of quitting the farm and the valley, and returning to his own home. " There may be enemies on the watch for you on all sides."

" I have seen no one afoot these many days, Diarmid, within many a mile of here," replied Rob Roy, " and you know that if my enemies were busy they would not travel singly, but in large companies, such as could easily be sighted afar off."

It was Rob Roy's custom every evening to ascend the hill opposite the house, and to walk on, a distance of about two miles, until he reached a lonely cairn, built upon the highest ground in all the neighbourhood. From the top of this he could spy into all the valleys on every side of him. In ancient times, before ever a Roman set foot in Britain, the cairn had perhaps been the watch-tower of a savage tribe; or it may merely have been the burial-place of a chief, or an altar to some heathen god; but, at all

events, it now served as a look-out post for Rob Roy, the outlawed chief of the MacGregors, who needed to see his way clear before him before setting out upon a journey in any direction.

" I will walk up with you to the cairn," said Diarmid, " while the sun is still up, so that we may make sure that there are no armed bands roving amid the hills."

Accordingly, Rob Roy and the young farmer set out, crossed the valley, and breasted the hill. When they reached the lofty plateau at the top of the hill it was a fine prospect that unfolded itself on all sides of them—mountains, and valleys, and winding rivers, with here and there a white farmhouse. The spot was far, however, from any town, and it seemed to be the centre of a vast, depopulated world.

Diarmid's keen eyes searched the valleys on all sides. There was no sign of rising dust, such as would accompany men on the march on any of the roads. There were no camp fires on any mountain spur, no roaming figures amid the heather.

" I think I may go which way I will," said Rob Roy, " and see nothing stirring but my own shadow. I will go home, Diarmid. I thank you for your hospitality, but I have business to do at home. Every way is clear, as you see."

" Bide a bit," said the younger man, " let us climb the cairn. We cannot spy into every glen from here."

So they walked on towards the great tower of unhewn stone which rose amidst the heather before them.

As they neared it Diarmid's eyes widened with wonder. He grasped Rob Roy's arm.

" What ails ye, Diarmid ? " said Rob Roy.

" Look ! Look ! I think the fairies have been at work, chief. There are strange signs on the cairn, splashes of blood, as I think."

They approached nearer to the pile of stones. Certainly there were strange signs and symbols on the cairn, which had never been there before. They were not rude splashes of colour, as Diarmid had thought, but crudely painted pictures.

On the face of the cairn confronting them were two red arrows. One pointed to the east, and in front of the barb of the arrow was a roughly-fashioned picture of a broadsword; the other pointed to the west, and in front of it was a picture which was evidently intended to represent a gun.

On another face of the cairn was an arrow pointing due south, and before it a red design which puzzled both Rob Roy and Diarmid. By a stretch of the imagination it might be supposed to represent a woman.

Diarmid's face wore an awed look.

"This is not canny," he said, "there is a meaning in all this, and I think the fairies have done it."

"Pshaw! It is the work of some idle callant who has been amusing himself here," said Rob Roy.

"And who would trouble to climb here to paint childish pictures that had no meaning? If this be not the work of fairies it is the work of enemies. These signs have some meaning, I doubt not, and will serve to guide your enemies."

"Why my enemies, Diarmid?"

"What strangers would come hither except the men who are watching for you? I have seen no strangers here these many years. It is not a place where men would come pleasuring."

"I will read these signs," said Rob Roy, laughing. "They are the work of some wayfaring Southron, a Lowlander, or perhaps an Englishman, and they signify that there is war to the east and war to the west, but to the south there is domestic happiness, typified, as you see, by the figure of a woman."

Diarmid shook his head. "Would any man, English or Lowland, carry with him a pail of paint?"

"Ay, he may be some wandering sign-painter."

"He will make no bread at his trade, then. There is no skill in these daubs."

"Well, then, the fairies have done them, as you say. But how shall we interpret them?" said Rob Roy, jestingly.

"They may be a warning to you. You must not go east or west or south."

"I think I may go south, Diarmid. I never feared a lassie yet, though this should be an ill-favoured one to judge her by her portrait."

But though Rob Roy laughed and jested, Diarmid was grave and gloomy. He felt sure that those strange signs held some meaning, and were meant to convey a message to Rob Roy's enemies, or perhaps to Rob Roy himself.

"Come home with me again, chief," he said, "until some of the lads can muster there to accompany you back to the Eagle's Nest."

"I will come back with you," said Rob Roy, no less gravely, "and take my supper with you, Diarmid, but after that I will go on my way. And since I may come to the Eagle's Nest soonest by turning to the west, I will go up the valley."

"There is danger that way," said Diarmid.

"There is danger all ways," said Rob Roy, "but I trust in God and my own right arm that have preserved me through many dangers."

It was near midnight when Rob Roy, fully armed and alone, left his kinsman's house behind him, and marched, in the silver moonlight, up the valley, intending, when he reached the end of it, to turn in a southerly direction, and so, after fifteen miles hard walking, to reach the vicinity of his mountain fastness.

CHAPTER III.

To East and to West.

It was two o'clock in the morning, clear and still, and the full moon threw sharply-cut shadows of rock and bush athwart Rob Roy's path.

He was near the narrow end of the valley when a stag rose from the heather close before him, and went speeding away, lightly crashing through brake and bramble. In the stillness of the night its rustling movements were plainly audible for some little while, and other ears than Rob Roy's heard the sounds it made.

Soon Rob Roy's quick eye detected on the slope of the ground to the right, and in advance of him, a little shelter built of furze-bushes.

"Oho!" he thought, "who bides here? Some deer-hunter, or roving gipsy, or——"

His reflections were cut short by the loud bang of a gun, not many yards distant from him, and at the same instant something struck the targe, or shield, he was carrying a terrific blow, so that he spun round and fell. In another few seconds he was up again, crouching, with sword drawn, through the heather, and the war-cry of the Campbells greeted his ears—a shrill note of menace.

"That will be Campbell of Glen

Ruthin," thought the MacGregor, " the only branch of the clan that is hostile to me."

And then, across the valley in front of him, he saw a line of swordsmen drawn to bar his way. Campbell of Glen Ruthin had not embarked upon his enterprise without bringing some of his retainers to aid him. But for the stag, which had roused them, Rob Roy might have passed them as they slept.

He raised the war-cry of Clan Gregor, and advanced impetuously upon the nearest man, who turned and drew quickly back. Rob Roy saw his intent —to draw him on till his fellows surrounded him—so he halted. Then he dropped to the ground, and drew his two pistols and cocked them.

A bonnet showing above a bush made an easy mark in the moonlight. He fired, and the bonnet disappeared. Then he changed his position, crawling out of sight behind the bushes, and a shower of lead whistled above him, a volley of reports rattled noisily in front of him.

For one instant Campbell of Glen Ruthin sprang up, and Rob Roy fired at him with his second pistol. He yelled a curse at the chief, whose bullet had grazed him, and fell out of sight again. Then Rob Roy heard him cry to his men to advance and slay " the red thief of a MacGregor." But no onslaught followed ; the men hung back ; only Rob Roy heard the rattle of ramrods being driven home, and knew that a volley awaited him if he himself advanced.

It was of no use to go on ; he could never get out of the valley alive if he did so. Bravery degenerates into the merest folly when it faces hopeless odds, unless honour is at stake. In this case Rob Roy's honour was not at stake ; he merely wished to get home ; he was fighting for no great cause ; he was simply opposed by a petty and spiteful enemy who was intent upon his assassination. So, being of a mind to disappoint Campbell of Glen Ruthin, the chief turned and crawled stealthily away, leaving the Campbells waiting and watching for the slightest stir in the heather, which would be a sign for them to loose off their volley. The sign was never given them ; they grew numbed, lying there in the cold dawn, while Rob Roy was tramping briskly back to Diarmid.

He reached the latter's house at sunrise, and Diarmid was pleased to welcome him back again.

"The fairies were right, Diarmid," said Rob Roy. "There's war to the west."

"Ay," said Diarmid, "then the red arrow was a hint to Campbell to hold the western end of the valley, with ball and powder. There was a gun painted, ye'll remember."

"So there was, Diarmid ; and Campbell's gun was surely aimed. My targe was struck."

He raised the shield as he spoke, and noticed for the first time that there was a bullet embedded in it.

Diarmid picked it out with the point of his skian dhu.

"A siller bullet!" he said. "Man, ye've had a narrow escape." For a silver bullet was supposed never to miss its mark.

"I'll try my luck going east to-night," said Rob Roy.

"'Deed, ye shall do no such thing. Just bide here till the fools gang hame. There was another arrow that pointed east, ye ken."

"Well, it pointed to a sword. If my enemies meet me steel to steel I can win through. No man can be sure of getting scatheless through a storm of bullets, especially when some of them be silver."

All day long Diarmid was urgent in his persuasions to the chief not to risk another adventure. But Rob Roy laughed at the symbols painted on the cairn, swore that they had no reference to him at all, and that he could get home by leaving the valley at its eastern extremity, although this would involve a longer journey round the hills.

At eleven o'clock at night he set off once again in the bright moonlight, but as he drew further and further away from Diarmid's house, he kept a sharp watch, a sharper watch than he had kept on the preceding night.

He was near the end of the valley when a tall figure suddenly rose from the heather, a sword flashed in the moonlight, and Rob Roy caught it on the edge of his targe.

Then he skipped back, unsheathed his claymore, and shouted, " Come on, John Grahame, if you wish your flesh to make a meal for the eagles."

His shock-headed enemy gave a fierce, mocking laugh, and approached him.

They circled about one another, wary and watchful, each waiting for a chance of running in and striking his enemy on some unguarded place.

At length Grahame made a quick leap, and his great sword descended in a slashing blow at Rob Roy's shoulder.

The sword struck the face of the targe, however, and Rob Roy's point grazed Grahame's left ear, which began to bleed profusely. The wounded giant cursed volubly, and then, with teeth clenched, struck again at the MacGregor, who caught the blow on his claymore.

Then the swords clashed together continually.

There was skill, as well as rude strength, however, behind those terrific blows. Brains and eyes were at work as well as muscles, and so it happened that for some minutes neither contestant harmed the other.

But at last Grahame made a lunge which Rob Roy failed to parry, for he made a similar attack at the same moment. Each man staggered back and fell. The heavens spun round, and Rob Roy felt himself whirled into darkness.

When he recovered he saw his enemy lying at a little distance from him.

"I must make sure he's dead," he thought, "or I'm no safe lying here. He'll stick his little knife into me if he can, when he comes round."

He sat up, but immediately sank back again, and fainted away. When he opened his eyes once more Diarmid was bending over him.

"Where's Grahame?" asked Rob Roy.

"Thank heaven, ye're no killed."

"I'm no killed, Diarmid, but I've lost much blood, and am weak as a kitten. Ah, that's better. I'm my own man again now," he added, after a draught of mountain dew from Diarmid's flask. "But where's Grahame?"

"Losh! who kens—or cares? He was crawling towards ye when I came up, with his skian dhu. I thought he was badly hurt at first, but when he saw me he rose and ran awa'. He would have been upon you, and his knife in your heart, I think, but that he thought you might be shamming, so he crept towards you warily."

"He swooned, as I did, at first."

"Ay, but he can walk again, as you

can. And it's back again to my house that ye'll walk, Rob Roy, and weel I wish that you'd take warning by the pictures on the cairn, for ye're girdled round with murderers."

Leaning upon Diarmid, the chief managed, after a painful and toilsome march, to reach the farmhouse again. And for some days he had, perforce, to take Diarmid's advice, and remain within doors.

However, his hardy frame suffered but slightly from loss of blood. He swore that John Grahame was a skilful surgeon, who had bled him, and thereby given him new strength. And the wound was scarcely healed when he began to talk once more of starting upon his perilous journey home.

"The valley is a narrow way," he said, "where one may easily walk into an ambush. I'll go over the hill to the south, where one cannot be surprised by sudden attack."

"Ye'll bide here till some of your lads come to fetch you," said Diarmid, gruffly.

CHAPTER IV.

TAVERN GOSSIP.

Rob Roy did not wait for his men to come and escort him home. No appointment had been made with them to meet him at Diarmid's, although he had thought that some of them might foregather at his hiding-place. But his wound grew well, he was tired of inaction, and he decided to set out for home across the hills. Grahame and Campbell might yet be lurking at either end of the valley, so he would strike due south.

"Man, I'm afeard," said Diarmid, when Rob Roy was actually preparing to start. "The red arrows mean mischief to you."

"I've escaped the sword and the gun," laughed Rob Roy, "and shall I fall a victim to a woman? If the signs mean aught, which I doubt, they mean that there is safety to the south."

But Diarmid shook his head. "Many a braw fellow that fears not lead or steel has been brought to naught by a woman. Think of Samson and Delilah."

"Fie upon you, Diarmid! Am I some beardless laddie to be caught by every roving, roguish eye that looks at me kindly ? I that have a wife of my own and sons as tall as myself nearly ? "

But Diarmid still shook his head.

"Oh, beware o' the woman, chief," he said, gravely.

And so, for the third time Rob Roy set out, climbing, upon this occasion, the hill in front of the house.

Again he travelled by night, but this time there was no moon, which seemed to render his journey more safe. By the cairn he paused; the stars gave sufficient light for him to see the symbols painted on the stones. They had not been effaced; indeed, there had been an addition to one of them : the woman now held in her red right hand what was, presumably, intended to represent a dagger.

Rob Roy halted by the cairn and pondered. Who was the unknown person who haunted this lonely hilltop and, after the manner of savage men, wrote messages of doubtful meaning in pictures?

For Rob Roy was convinced by now that these crude pictures had a meaning, although he was not sure that they were intended to speak to him. It was true that he had been in the habit of visiting the cairn every day to look out for enemies, and this fact might have become known. But there was no one save Diarmid and the folks of his household dwelling within many miles of the cairn. Who would trouble to walk miles over the hills to do him this service—if it was intended as a warning to him ?

"These are signs by which my enemies speak to one another," he thought. "And yet, why cannot they meet and talk together ? "

Finally, with a careless laugh, he left the cairn, and strode on through the darkness.

The sun was up when he reached the first cluster of houses that lay in his path. This was a small village with an inn, a shoeing forge, a kirk, and about a dozen or so cottages.

Rob Roy disdained to go out of his way to avoid passing the village. It was the home of peaceable people, and if any enemy chanced to be resting at the inn he was ready armed to fight or to threaten him.

He thought, however, that he had got out of the circle of his enemies. They would scarcely attempt anything against him in a village where he could call men to his aid. As he was an outlaw, men

might, quite legitimately, stand by and see him murdered. But woe betide the village or town in which this was done ! Its inhabitants might be quite sure that the slogan of Clan Gregor would ring through their streets, and that their houses and ricks would be given over to the flames by the wild MacGregors, in a very short time.

So Rob Roy strode into the village street with a feeling of perfect security.

He bade the blacksmith good-morning, walked into the inn, and broke his fast. There was no one present who could be regarded as an enemy. The only people about the place, indeed, were the innkeeper himself—an old Highlander who tried to keep on good terms with men of all clans—and a little boy, who had been sent in by a neighbour to buy a noggin of whisky, and who went out after a shy glance at the chief, whose bright tartan seemed to take his fancy.

Tired by his night march, Rob Roy fell asleep in the ingle-nook, and slept on till noon, when an old man hobbled into the room.

"Neebour," he said, to the innkeeper, " have ye heard the tidings ? Losh ! those dour Campbells are an ill race to dwell amongst—the whey-faced Whigamores ! "

" Softly, Andrew," said the innkeeper, winking and jerking his thumb in the direction of Rob Roy, "the Campbells are a fine, warlike race, and the Duke is a grand man indeed. But what have ye heard o' the Campbells noo ? "

"Hech ! They're for stealing awa' Duncan MacGregor's daughter, and Duncan has been a' the nicht praying them to gang awa', and pointing at them with his gun. But they will no gang without the lassie."

" And what would they with the lassie, Andrew ? "

" Oh, they're for marrying her to Robin Campbell, a poor feckless body, as ye ken, and they'll do it, too."

There was a stir in the ingle-nook. Rob Roy arose with a frown on his face.

" Whence came these Campbells that dare put an affront upon a MacGregor ? " he said.

The old gossip looked startled, and then smiled grimly. Here was a fine piece of sport ! The chief of the MacGregors would himself take a hand in this quarrel, and there would be a fine story to tell the neighbours presently —that was what his smile seemed to imply.

" What Campbells are these ? " Rob Roy demanded again.

" Oh, it's just Robin—Robin of G gyle, and his brither, and others of his kinsmen."

" I never heard his name before, but if he has any care for his own interests he will, maybe, listen to a word or two from Rob Roy MacGregor, who is a friend of the Duke's."

" Ay, the Duke is a graund man," said the old gossip.

" The Duke knows better than to affront a MacGregor, or to let his clansmen do the like. Where is this MacGregor's house, that ye speak of ? I know of no MacGregor's hereabouts."

The old man plucked his sleeve and led him to the open door of the inn.

" I should not have spoken of the matter before him," he said, softly, meaning the innkeeper, " he's ower fond of the Campbells, ye ken. Duncan MacGregor bides out away yonder. Ye'll take the path up past the sheep-fold and pass between the two rocks you spy up yonder, and so on till you reach the headless cross. And then ye'll take the left hand track for a mile and a bit, when ye'll come to Duncan's house, and I hope ye'll not find the lassie stolen awa', for Robin Campbell is a poor feckless boy, and no a fit husband for a bonny lass like Duncan's daughter."

" If she is stolen away so much the worse for Campbell of Gledgyle. If they are still about the house I shall make the peace between them and my clansmen."

So saying, the chief stepped out quickly in the direction indicated. Although it was quite usual for Highlanders to steal their brides, it did not follow that this bride was willing to be stolen. The matter wanted looking into. Rob Roy thought that he could, by a few words, make peace between the two parties, for his commands would have weight with most of the Campbells, who knew him for a friend of the Duke's. Campbell of Ruthin was an exception.

" But how comes a MacGregor to be settled here ? " he asked himself. " I have no knowledge of him. He may give me shelter for awhile, and he may know if there are any wandering Murrays or Grahames hereabouts."

So he climbed on, past the sheepfold, between the lofty rocks that had been pointed out to him, and so on to the headless cross, which, like the cairn, was a relic of times of which history contains no account.

" Andrew," said the innkeeper, standing at the door of his house, and shading his eyes, as he watched Rob Roy's toilsome ascent of the hill, " the MacGregor is no on the richt path for Duncan MacGregor's house. Did ye tell him wrang ? "

" 'Deed, no," said the old man, smiling craftily, as he gazed into the fire, " but it's too late to call him back the noo. Robin will get awa' with the lassie, I fear. But, losh ! She may be willing for all I ken or care. I'll tak' a sup of whisky, man."

" You've come by a braw lot of siller, Andrew," said the innkeeper, who noticed that the old man, usually so poor, was counting a handful of silver.

" Aye, I've been at the long stocking," said the old man. " I've hoarded it ower long. My span is nearly run, and I'm thinking there's no drinking hereafter."

The innkeeper filled a glass and looked thoughtful.

CHAPTER V.

IN PRISON AND OUT AGAIN.

By the headless cross Rob Roy came to a halt. It stood on high, level ground, a dreary wind-swept waste.

" I'm to take the left hand track, and to follow it for a mile and a bit," he thought. The track was plainly marked, there could be no mistaking it ; so he struck into it, and hurried along, hoping to aid his persecuted clansman.

In due time he came into sight of a strongly-built granite house, set in a hollow on the braeside, where it was sheltered from the cold winds of the north and east.

No glint of Campbell tartan showed anywhere near it.

" I fear the rogues have prevailed," he thought ; " ay, the house door is open, and there's none about. They've carried off the lassie, and her father's gone after her, if, indeed, it's no worse."

He approached the deserted dwelling, only hoping that he might not find its tenant lying lifeless across his own threshold. The Campbells would not willingly compass such a lawless deed as murder perhaps, but when the blood is hot and blows are being exchanged, mischances may occur that were never intended to happen.

Rob Roy crossed the threshold of the house and called aloud to know if there was anyone indoors. No response came to his summons. He noticed that the furniture in the room he had entered had been thrown about, as if there had been a tussle. The door of a back room stood ajar, and something which he could see lying on the floor of it attracted his attention. It was a woman's kerchief.

He strode into the room, which was empty. Instantly the door was clapped to, and he heard the sound of bolts being shot. His hand instinctively closed upon his sword-hilt; but a man cannot fight the air. He was alone in the room. For a moment he was bewildered; he thought that the rascally Campbells had thus imprisoned him. Then he saw that he had walked unsuspectingly into a trap.

There were no Campbells concerned in the business at all, and this was not the house of a MacGregor. The old man at the inn was in the pay of some enemy. Why had he led him out of earshot of the innkeeper before pointing out the way to Duncan MacGregor's house—why, unless he intended to deceive?

It was the sound of a mocking laugh that convinced Rob Roy that a trap had been laid for him—a woman's laugh. His mind instantly reverted to the red figure painted upon the lonely cairn.

But the woman was speaking to him.

"Bide there awhile, MacGregor," she said, "I'm glad to welcome you to my house, and there'll be company for ye soon. Eh, but to think of the braw MacGregor being taken prisoner by a woman! There'll be many a laugh in Scotland over this."

"I'll not bandy words with the jade," thought Rob Roy. "Let her have her laugh. Maybe it will be my turn later."

He began to investigate his prison. It was a small, bare room. The door was heavy and obviously strongly secured on the outside; the window was small and strongly barred, but for all that it did not seem to the Chief to be a very formidable prison. He might, given sufficient time, work

a hole in the door with his dagger, and so thrust his arm out and pull back the bolts.

No sooner had he thought of this than he began to try the point of his dagger on the door. The blade was keen and finely-tempered, but the door was of solid heart of oak. It would be a long job, and the dagger might break. He would need both patience and caution to accomplish the task.

While he was considering it, he heard the ring of footsteps in the flagged passage outside.

"Where is he, where is he? So ye've trapped the fox! Old Andrew sent the boy to tell me he had come this way."

Rob Roy's brow darkened. That was the voice of Geordie Murray.

"He's in the still-room," said the woman. "Have a care. He's armed."

"Armed! Ye fool! Ye feckless jade, to send him in there armed. Could ye no have got him to sit down and drink with ye, and think he was in a friend's house and lay by his arms?"

There was much wrangling after this, and the prisoner heard many men's voices being raised in dispute.

"You're four to one, you're four to one," cried the woman, shrilly and tauntingly. "Now, let me see who dares unbar the door, and I'll gie my hand to the bravest among you."

"Have done, you jade," said Murray, in the tone of a jealous man. "I'll have no light talking of that sort."

"Now I call that a fair bargain," said another man, noisily. "Will you hold to your bargain, widow? It would make it worth a man's while to cross swords with the MacGregor."

Murray swore angrily, and Rob Roy guessed now whose house he was in. It was the house of the Widow Macduff, whose husband had been killed in an affray with some of the MacGregors, whom she therefore hated indiscriminately; he had heard that she was betrothed to dark Geordie Murray. They had evidently laid their trap for him carefully, employing the crafty old man, Andrew, to watch for him in the village, and probably the small boy also, who had gone out of the inn a short while before Andrew entered it.

There was more wrangling outside, and then suddenly a small panel in the door was slipped back, disclosing a grating, and, behind the grating, the sinister face of George Murray, with the ugly scarred nose.

"So we've caged you, MacGregor," he said, "and caged you surely. Eh! you may laugh, but you'll be crying out for bread and water soon."

By way of reply Rob Roy took out a flask he carried with him and raised it to his lips. "Here's to the time when we next cross swords, Murray," he said.

"That may be at Armageddon, Mac-Gregor, when the elect do battle with the wicked; but it'll no be in this world," replied George Murray.

The panel was slipped to, and Rob Roy understood that his enemies intended to starve him to death, or to postpone opening the door until he was too weak to lift his sword.

However, he was far from feeling any despair at his situation yet. He hoped, for one thing, that the woman's taunts would drive the men to unbar the door, and then, although the odds against him would be four to one, he felt confident that he could hew his way back to liberty.

The hours dragged on slowly. Like a caged lion the Chief paced the floor of his narrow prison. He had abandoned all idea of extricating himself by cutting through the door, for it was apparently cased with iron on the outside. He had driven his dagger deeply into the oak, and the point had been stayed and blunted by metal when two inches deep in the wood. The window, even if the bars were removed, would be an impracticable exit. It was too small for a man to squeeze through. But he had not abandoned hope. The woman might goad the men into unfastening the door. He heard her laughing, jeering, taunting the men with cowardice. He heard Murray's voice often raised in anger. One of the men wished to hold the widow to her careless promise to give her hand to the man who should unbar the door and confront the prisoner, and the widow's affianced lover resented this.

"They'll come to blows yet," thought Rob Roy.

But the twilight fell, and they grew quieter. It grew dark, and all was silence, until, late at night, he heard the woman bid her guests good-night, and ascend the stairs. The men were evidently going to remain in the house.

Cold, hungry, and dispirited by the monotony of the long hours, Rob Roy

wrapped his plaid about him, and lay down on the hard floor to sleep.

He woke from an uneasy slumber, and his senses were all immediately on the alert. Someone was drawing back the bolts of the door. The sound was scarcely perceptible, for great caution was being used. A bolt was being drawn little by little. There was more than one bolt and the operation took a long time; and all the while Rob Roy, lying against the wall near the door, was as noiselessly unsheathing his claymore.

A new moon shed sufficient light into the room to see by. The prisoner saw when the door, at last unbarred, began to move inwards. It moved inch by inch, then a head appeared; the nocturnal visitant was looking in to see if the prisoner slept. Rob Roy did not stir.

Then, with quick, gliding steps the widow came towards him, in her hand an uplifted dagger.

Rob Roy rose, and she gave a smothered cry, scarcely more than a gasp. His sword gleamed, its point towards her; she could not approach near enough to strike him.

"Were you a man," whispered the Chief, "you should die. I am guiltless of your husband's blood. Now stand aside."

Fearful of his sword, in spite of his words, she drew back, breathing quickly. Rob Roy was out of the room in a twinkling, and at the same moment the woman screamed. The passage was instantly full of armed men, and Rob Roy struck at random in the dark.

Clink, clank, sword played upon sword, or beat the walls of the passage in vain efforts to find a living enemy. Someone bellowed for a light, and one of the men hastily lit a candle in the room where they had been lying. The light streamed out into the passage, and Rob Roy dashed to the staircase. Standing on the lowest stair he had his enemies all before him. In the passage he might have been attacked treacherously from behind as well as in front.

And now the Chief was confident of escape; four swords threatened him, but the men were crowded together awkwardly, and none of them had Rob Roy's length of reach. With a thrust here, and a thrust there, he kept his enemies back, until one, seizing what he thought to be an opportune moment, stooped and tried to get in under his guard. Rob Roy was ready for him; he shortened his sword, and drove the point into his chest just in time to stop him. The man reeled back, and for an instant his comrades gave him their attention. In that moment Rob Roy was up the stairs; he dashed into one of the rooms, took up a chair, and shivered the window to atoms, and so dropped fifteen feet to the ground.

The door of the house was thrown open with a great clatter. Three of his enemies ran out, shouting loudly. They pursued him across a mile of heather, before he bethought himself that he was going in the wrong direction for home. He was, in fact, running back along the way he had come in the morning.

Accordingly, he pulled up, and, with sword drawn, considered whether he should attempt to pass through the line of oncoming enemies.

To his surprise he saw that they had been reinforced. Their cries had brought friends to their aid, who must have been lurking near the widow's house, and a long-extended line of kilted swordsmen was advancing towards him.

Famished and spent by fighting as he was, he could not face that large band with much hope of success. If he tried to break through the line a dozen men would converge upon the place where he made the attempt. To drop in the heather and hide while they went by would be impossible, for they had kept him in view from the first.

There was nothing for it but flight, for the present. He did not wish to return yet again to Diarmid's house, although he could think of no other place where he could shelter safely, in all the countryside, except under that hospitable but yet distant roof. His enemies would, he thought, leave him unmolested there, for any length of time, for they wished to kill him secretly, when there was no possibility of the story of their deed reaching the ears of the MacGregors. An assault upon a stout farmhouse, besides being a perilous undertaking, could scarcely remain unchronicled in the neighbourhood.

But although there might be safety with Diarmid, the Chief's pride revolted at the thought of beating a retreat thither for the third time. He was

obliged, however, to continue his flight in that direction, for his enemies were following him hotly, with fierce, exultant cries.

CHAPTER VI.

A Hot Pursuit.

Down the mountain side went Rob Roy, into the silent moonlit street of the sleeping village.

"I might tarry at the inn," he thought, "but though they would not attack me there they would surround the village. I should be in no better case than at Diarmid's, and worse housed into the bargain." For although this village inn was superior to the lonely buddel or drinking-shop, five miles away, where Rob Roy's enemies foregathered, its accommodation was rough and poor, and its customers, as he had already had proof, in league with Murray.

So he passed the inn and went out at the end of the village street, Murray and his following still after him. The villagers wisely kept their windows shuttered when they heard the clatter of armed men outside. It would be dangerous to meddle on either side.

But, although they pretended to hear nothing, the story of the great MacGregor's flight from his enemies was buzzed about next morning, in the village and the neighbourhood, and discussed in whispers in farmhouse and tavern.

After leaving the village behind him, Rob Roy had to cross a river, which he did by a small stone bridge, and then he was fairly on his way back to Diarmid again. His enemies followed him, to the number of seven or eight, across the bridge, and into the hilly country beyond the river. There was no retracing his steps now, for the bridge, the only one for miles, would be guarded.

Rob Roy still led the way by some distance, but his enemies, owing to the bright moonlight, were able to keep him well in sight for some time. At last he came to a place where there was a narrow cave, at the foot of a rocky cliff. There was only room in the entrance of it for one man; to any man standing in it an army of swordsmen would be no more peril than a solitary enemy, for only one man would be able to attack him at a time, while the others remained spectators of the fight.

Into this narrow fissure Rob Roy ran, and turned and faced the entry, standing a yard or two within the cave.

"Now they must attack me singly," he thought, "and if they dare do that, I will take them all in turn, for I am more than a match for any one of them."

He waited for a short while, recovering breath for the coming conflict. He had his pistol in his left hand, his sword in his right; his enemies had followed him so hurriedly from the house that they had not, he believed, thought to bring their pistols with them.

He saw them dash past him, hot and breathless, calling to one another.

"Where is he? He dropped in the heather," cried one.

"We have him now. He must be close at hand," panted Murray.

For awhile they did not espy the cave, and all this time Rob Roy was recovering his breath, while they were getting more and more flustered in their impatient search for him.

Then, suddenly, Murray appeared at the mouth of the cave. With a snarl of rage he started back, taken by surprise. Rob Roy raised his pistol, fired, but fired a second too late. Murray had drawn aside.

And now a shrill colloquy took place outside, each man reproaching the others for having brought no weapons but swords.

In the midst of it a tall swordsman blundered into the mouth of the fissure, and struck violently at Rob Roy, who had had no time to reload his pistol. He was in time, however, to ward off the heavy blow of the swinging claymore, and he immediately afterwards cut the man across the arm.

The fellow sprang back and out of sight, cursing volubly.

"There's no room to make play with your sword in there," he said, as he held his arm out to be bound up.

"The MacGregor seems to find room," replied another man.

"Ay!" shouted Rob Roy, "there's room for two men to stand face to face here, and no more. How like ye such odds? Geordie Murray, come on, and I'll teach you a new trick of fence. You're but a clumsy swordsman."

Murray muttered a curse between his teeth; he had too great a respect for Rob Roy's swordsmanship to venture lightly into the cleft where the Chief stood with keen blade ready for cut or thrust.

But another rough fellow, after a stiff pull at the flask he carried, suddenly gripped his sword-hilt and rushed into the entry. There was a short, sharp clatter of swords, and the man backed out, and then staggered and fell, wounded in the shoulder.

"That makes two," shouted Rob Roy, "and I think you number seven. Who takes the next turn?"

After much muttering on the part of the men, two of them appeared at once in the narrow entry with swords advanced. The experiment was not a success. Two men could not squeeze in side by side, much less could they use their swords to any purpose Before they could back away again, which they did very precipitately, Rob Roy managed to hit one of them on the shin, inflicting a slight wound, which angered the recipient thereof greatly.

"And that makes three," he sang out. "I've bled three of ye like a good surgeon, and I hope that will abate your madness. But the maddest of ye all is Murray. Why don't you come to the surgeon, Murray?"

But this taunt would not provoke Murray to daring. He had told his friends, Grahame and Campbell, upon the occasion of their plotting together, that the man who came within reach of Rob Roy's sword was likely never to handle sword again. He did not mean to run needless risks.

"Gang awa' hame, Jamie," he said, "and bring a brace o' pistols."

This suggestion met with the approval of everyone except Rob Roy. In a duel with pistols he would stand less chance of escaping scot-free. But, then, he would not remain where he was to be shot at; of that he was resolved.

Hastily he loaded his own pistol, leaned out of his narrow den, and speeded the departing Jamie with a bullet, which, unfortunately, went wide of the mark aimed at.

With a hurried glance Rob Roy then took stock of his enemies. Two of them were patching up their slight but painful wounds, the more severely wounded man was lying in the heather, and the three whole men left were standing, with swords drawn, their faces turned towards him, surprised by his pistol-shot.

"I've a bullet for each of you!" he sang out. "Stand where ye are, my laddies."

This, of course, was precisely what they did not do. They retired behind a rock, wounded men and all, before Rob Roy could again reload his pistol.

And now he had a fair chance of getting away. He would go out, bring down one man with his pistol, and then there would be but two swordsmen to follow him. He would lead them on for a bit, and then turn and take them both together. Two to one was no desperate odds to Rob Roy, although three to one would be perilous to any man. He waited a minute or two, after loading his pistol, and then walked calmly out of his shelter, and ran softly over the heather a few yards before he was seen

Then there was a yell; three men advanced, but one fell when Rob Roy fired. After that he turned and ran. Presently he faced out.

"And now for the other two brave fellows!" he said. But they numbered four instead of two. The man whose leg had been touched by his sword-point was able to follow, after all. The man who had dropped when he fired his pistol had only done so to escape the bullet, not because the bullet had struck him.

This put a different complexion upon matters; Rob Roy was obliged to continue his flight.

It was now daylight again, and there seemed little hope of being able to disappear from the eyes of his vigilant enemies. He hoped to be able to fire them out.

Mile after mile he ran, before the pursuit slackened perceptibly. But it was slackening at last, and Rob Roy thought he saw the way clear before him back to Diarmid's house—since he could do no better than return thither—when to his dismay he saw the glint of Campbell tartan on the hill in front of him, and then Campbell and Ruthin and George Murray hailed one another, and Rob Roy was between two parties of enemies.

He changed his direction instantly, darting off to the right, the Campbells having been a little to the left and in advance of him before.

He halted for a moment at a mountain stream to quench his thirst, and then went on again, with nine or ten men now following him, although Murray and his companions lagged far behind the new-comers. But the Campbells were fresh and resolute, and, what was worse, carried muskets.

He kept out of musket range, however, though not without sore effort, for he was growing very weary.

Suddenly he changed his direction slightly, making for higher ground. The pursuit had taken place hitherto along a valley bottom, and then up a gentle slope and along the side of a mountain.

Rob Roy saw that a thick, white cloud was rolling over the mountain top, enveloping its summit.

Up he went, up and up, and now a musket bullet went close past his feet. But a minute later he was in the thick bank of fog, and his enemies could only fire random and unaimed shots at him if they fired at all.

Still, he ascended a little way, and then threw himself down, breathing heavily, among some rocks. He could scarcely see his hand in front of him. The cloud had saved him, for the time at all events; it might, of course, roll away.

As he lay among the rocks, with his pistol ready, he heard his pursuers pass close beside him, cautiously and quietly, sometimes evidently blundering into one another.

At length a man showed, gigantic, shadowy, within a few feet of him. He stood and listened intently for any sound. He was completely at Rob Roy's mercy, but unless the fellow noticed him Rob Roy did not wish to fire, for the sound might guide others to him.

There was a minute of suspense and silence; after that the man vanished into the fog again, all sounds gradually died away in the distance, and, overcome by exhaustion, Rob Roy fell asleep.

When he awoke he wondered at first where he was. The clouds had dispersed, the sun had set long ago, for he had slept many hours. Below him was the valley, above him were the twinkling stars, for the moon had not yet risen.

He rose, conscious of the fact that he was ravenously hungry. There was certainly nothing for it now but to go straight back to Diarmid, and prepare to make a fresh start again.

His flight had taken him some miles out of his way, so he travelled all through the small hours at the best speed he was capable of.

"I'll warrant Murray and Campbell are putting their heads together to think how they can do me fresh mischief," he thought as he marched along, "but it's little I care for any of them. I'll be back in the Eagle's Nest soon, and no man in Scotland can harm me there."

So he went on confidently enough, and a little before sunrise came into view at last of the cairn of unhewn stones from which he had been accustomed to look out for his enemies. The morning air was hazy, and the cairn yet showed but dimly across the heathery space between it and Rob Roy, when something seemed to detach itself from the stone-heap and glide swiftly away.

Rob Roy uttered an exclamation of astonishment.

"Yon's my unknown friend!" he said. "I must come up with him, and ask why he delivers his messages in this strange fashion. Who is he, and what brings him up here, so far away from any man's dwelling save Diarmid's?"

He ran forward, but the grey, misty figure quickly disappeared. Rob Roy would not raise his voice, lest it might be no friend, but an enemy, and other enemies lurking within earshot.

He stared all about him, but could not see the figure again.

"I wish I could have caught the fellow," he thought, "then if he has aught to tell me he might have told it by word of mouth.

The sun rose, and the cairn stood out more clearly against the blue of the morning sky; the mists began to rise, but though Rob Roy looked hither and thither he could see no one moving in that solitary place.

"My unarmed friend is swift and nimble, it seems," he thought. "I would like fine to have a crack with him, for he seems to know the dark plans of Murray, and Grahame, and Campbell. And how comes he by that knowledge? Well, they plotted something fresh yestre'en, I'll swear. Haply he'll come to hear of that too. I wish I were safe housed at Diarmid's, with a good bowl of brose before me." At

the thought of good fare he hurried along more vigorously than before.

CHAPTER VII.
The Fourth Sign.

By the lonely cairn Rob Roy came to a halt. He saw the red arrow pointing south, and the crudely depicted female figure, and "Ay, my unknown friend," he said, "you were no in error; you've no made her well-favoured, and, by my troth, you were right. She's an ill jade to deal with."

He saw now, plainly enough, that the marks on the cairn were painted there as warnings to himself. The sword had threatened him in one direction, the gun in another, the woman with the dagger in the third direction; but how came the mysterious artist by his foreknowledge of these perils? Diarmid believed in fairies, but Rob Roy had just seen a man near the cairn.

His brow darkened a little when he thought again that he must go back to Diarmid, and confess himself beaten for the third time. The fourth attempt at escape from his girdle of enemies should, however, prove successful, and then, perhaps, a day of reckoning would come for them, and Campbell of Ruthin, and Grahame and all, should suffer from their late presumption.

"By St. Andrew, but what's this?"

The exclamation was drawn from Rob Roy by the sight of a fourth arrow. The paint was yet wet. The arrow pointed north, to Diarmid's house; and before it, a daub of still wet paint was the representation of a barrel.

In spite of his mystification Rob Roy burst into loud laughter.

"My unknown adviser will have me safe nowhere," he said to himself, "sword, bullet and dagger all threaten me in turn, and now, if I read the sign aright, I am warned that there is danger in Diarmid's whisky cask. Well, well, a Southron might find Highland hospitality a perilous thing, but I must run the risk of being killed by kindness, despite the warning of my invisible friend."

He climbed the cairn, and searched the country round on every side with his glance, in hopes of seeing the mysterious artist, who had left the hilltop so recently; but he saw no one.

An hour later he was recounting his adventures to Diarmid.

The latter was quite convinced now that the signs on the cairn were due to supernatural agency; the misty figure must be a phantom; but he could offer no interpretation of the fourth sign.

"It canna signify that there is danger in my house," he said, "but that there is some peril to the north of you. You must not gang north."

"That," said Rob Roy, "I am little likely to do. For one thing, my way lies not in that direction, and for another, I cannot climb the cliff behind your house. Have a care, Diarmid! If you are plotting to drown me in your rain barrel I shall find a way of getting the better of ye yet."

But although he made light of the matter, his friend Diarmid pondered deeply over this fresh mystery. The few men he employed about the farm were old retainers, tried and trusty; moreover, with one or two exceptions, they were MacGregors themselves, ready to die for their chief; there could be no peril to Rob Roy from within the household. But some peril threatened; the red arrows had given trustworthy warnings upon three occasions. The fourth arrow could not be disregarded.

Finally Diarmid came to the conclusion that an attack upon his house was intended, and he was careful about bolts and fastenings at night, and careful to keep all fire-arms loaded. He also had the farm hands to sleep in the house. But these were all elderly men, and Diarmid wished heartily that some of Rob Roy's young men—men of the kind he kept about him in the Eagle's Nest—would come in search of their chief, and escort him out of the reach of danger.

For two nights after Rob Roy's return to the house nothing untoward happened; upon the third night Rob Roy and Diarmid were sitting smoking tobacco in the kitchen where they took their meals. The farm hands were all asleep in their beds.

"I wish ye were well out of this, chief," said Diarmid. "The rogues will not hurt me, for they will leave this part of the country so soon as you be gone; but they've hemmed you round."

"They have that, Diarmid," replied Rob Roy, "but I'll make another march to-morrow. Grahame will have to let me pass this time."

"No, no," said Diarmid, "Grahame has got others with him by now. I doubt not, and in the narrow neck of the valley you cannot slip by unnoticed."

"Pshaw! I can deal with half a dozen like Grahame."

"Not if they have guns, chief. The finest swordsman in Scotland can do naught against an ounce of lead. 'Tis a sore pity gunpowder was ever invented. It makes a coward behind a wall the superior of a valiant man in the open. Bide here, chief, till your lads come to clear the valley of this rabble."

"You forget, Diarmid, that there is danger here, if the fairies are to be believed," said Rob Roy with a mischievous smile. "'Deed, and I thought you eyed the rain-barrel over earnestly to-day, and measured me against it with your eye, as if to see whether it would hold me. I'm not sure of your intentions, Diarmid."

"My intentions are to keep you from being over bold, and running into danger with your eyes shut, and single-handed," replied matter-of-fact Diarmid.

"Well, if you'll not put me in the rain-barrel I'll bide a wee, yet," replied Rob Roy, "and if my boys come to seek me we'll make a merry din in the valley, and out beyond the hills, too. The widow Macduff may haply need to look for another bridegroom than Geordie Murray. I have no love for a man who would have starved me. Hush! what's that?"

A sound, as of a rat gnawing, suddenly attracted their attention.

But "'Tis no rat," said Diarmid, hastily lighting a lantern. The sound was outside the house.

"Take your pistol, chief."

Diarmid held the lantern in one hand, and a pistol in the other, and went towards the door. Rob Roy passed in front of him, flung open the door, and the rays of the lantern streamed out into the darkness. Diarmid flashed the light here and there, and then almost dropped the lantern. Its rays fell for a moment upon a black figure that sprang up from the ground near the house and vanished into the darkness. Rob Roy ran out a little way and fired his pistol.

"Did ye see him?" said Diarmid, "Losh! whoever saw the like? Did ye notice his black jerkin and small clothes? 'Twas no man, chief."

Rob Roy laughed. Kilts were the customary wear in the Highlands, to be sure, but there was no reason why a man should not wear knee breeches and dress in black. The dark, attenuated, nimble figure, however, had certainly looked uncanny, viewed by the lantern's flickering light.

"Maybe it's my friend from the cairn," said Rob Roy, "and if that is so I am glad my aim was no surer. He's gone away. But what was he doing out here so near to the house?"

They examined the ground and found that the turf had been turned amidst some shrubs about five yards in front of the house. They inspected the turf closely, but could divine no reason why it had been cut. Squares of turf had been taken up, and put back again in their places. The man in black was a mysterious gardener, certainly.

After turning the turfs, and spending some time in useless wonder, Rob Roy and Diarmid returned to the house, much puzzled. That some danger threatened was beyond a doubt.

"We must sit up till daylight," said the chief, "and keep our pistols handy."

So pipes were refilled and glasses replenished, and the two MacGregors kept vigil till the sky was grey. But nothing further happened to puzzle or disturb them.

CHAPTER VIII.

A DISASTROUS BLOW.

The following night Rob Roy and his kinsman sat up until sleep overtook them as they rested in their chairs. Not a sound was audible outside so long as they were awake. They had patrolled the garden in the dark more than once, without seeing anything more of the mysterious gardener.

When they fell asleep, however, there were faint sounds outside—the sound of a spade being used, very cautiously, then a faint crash, as of something heavy falling.

After that there was a thud, beneath the floor of the kitchen, so it seemed. This woke Diarmid.

He sprang to his feet. "Did ye no hear it?" he cried.

Rob Roy also sprang up. The next instant both thought the end of the world had surely come. Fire and smoke and falling *débris* filled the room. An awful report deafened them. They were both hurled almost senseless to the ground, and choked in the sulphury darkness.

Grimed with powder-smoke, Diarmid rose to his feet. He tried to grope his way to the table where the tinder-box had been, but all familiar objects seemed to have disappeared. At that moment, however, one of the servants came in with a candle.

Its light revealed a room wrecked by explosion. The furniture was scattered all about the place. There was a yawning hole in one corner of the room, and another ragged opening in the outer wall of the room, beside the shattered window. Through this opening a man was peering, a man in black, with a grimed face. Diarmid deliberately picked up a pistol and shot him through the head.

Even in the confusion of the moment Rob Roy understood what had happened. The house had been undermined; the sign on the cairn was meant to represent a barrel of gunpowder, and the sounds they had heard had been made by the crafty miner at his work, the man whom Diarmid had shot.

When the smoke had cleared a little Rob Roy went to the opening in the wall, but quickly drew back.

"There are men outside," he said.

It was true. Tired of trying to catch him in the open, some of Rob Roy's enemies had determined to destroy him in the stout stronghold that harboured him. Unaware that they had not succeeded, they were preparing to enter the house through the hole the powder had torn, but the sight of their friend's body deterred them for a few moments.

Then a voice sounded. It was John Grahame's. "Follow me, I am going in."

The next instant the breach was attempted by two or three men. But Rob Roy had found his claymore. He slashed at John Grahame, who retired only just in time to save his life. Then a savage howl was raised by the angry men, who knew that the fourth attempt to take Rob Roy's life had failed.

"We must guard the breach. They

can get in no other way," said Rob Roy. "We are five strong men, and can surely keep them out."

Unfortunately this was not quite true. There were two strong men in the house, and three terrified old servants, whose tremulous fingers could hardly aim a musket.

"They must all die!" shouted Grahame, without the house, "or this will be carried to the ears of the MacGregors. Follow me again, and no skulking. The mine was ill-laid, more's the pity."

Diarmid stood at the window, where the shutters hung aslant from their hinges, ready to fire when the rush came. Rob Roy hastily placed a beam across the breach, so that the invaders must crawl under it or climb over it, according as the fancy took them. The servants were told to reload for Rob Roy and Diarmid.

The position was not a pleasant one. Owing to the breach the house was no longer an impregnable fortress, and Grahame and his band were very determined. If any man lived to tell how Diarmid's house had been undermined it would go ill with John Grahame. The MacGregors were numerous and dangerous. If the occupants of the house were all slain no one would be able to say that John Grahame had done it this mischief.

Diarmid fired from the window, and a man fell; five others crowded about the breach, and one ducked under the beam while a second fired over it. Rob Roy fired in reply, and the man who had fired staggered back. The second man retired hurriedly, and Grahame swore hotly in the darkness outside.

"They've gone round the corner of the house," announced Diarmid.

"Can they find their way in there?"

"No, the windows are all too small."

"They've but gone to recover breath."

"Ay! so I think."

This was true. There was silence, until suddenly a man appeared in the breach, to which he had crawled close against the wall of the house. He was up and in the room before Rob Roy could raise his musket to fire. Diarmid left the window, and struck at the fellow with the butt of his musket. The man, for his part, used his claymore. Rob Roy was about to assist Diarmid, when he saw the opening crowded again

with men struggling and pressing to get in. He fired his musket, and one man fell. Then he snatched up his claymore, and struck again at John Grahame, the only man who had the courage to remain. He drew aside. Rob Roy's sword descended upon the beam and stuck fast. Over this barrier flashed Grahame's sword, in a vicious thrust at the Chief's breast. But Rob Roy had stepped back, the thrust fell short, a servant handed him a gun, and Grahame retired after his men. The wounded had been pulled out of the breach.

Diarmid's opponent, meanwhile, was fighting desperately. Before Rob Roy could join in the affray and despatch him, he leapt to the window, and got through it; but Diarmid's musket butt descended on his back as he did so, and they heard him choking outside as he groped his way to his fellows.

"Man, Diarmid, we're doing fine," said Rob Roy; "there'll not be many of them left to hear the morning cocks crow, if they come again."

Certainly the attackers had fared but ill so far, but they were numerous; they could attack the house in shifts, one party resting while the other was busy. The defenders must be on the alert continually, with never an instant to spare for sleep or refreshment. If the siege continued very long the little garrison must eventually be tired out.

It was daybreak before another assault was made. A row of musket barrels showed above the barrier, and Rob Roy had barely time to drop to the ground before a volley was fired. Then he fired his musket, and, calling to Diarmid, rushed forward, sword in hand, just in time to keep out the invaders. One man, with his leg across the barrier, plied his claymore grimly, striving to climb over, but he only withdrew his leg in time to avoid losing it, for Diarmid's claymore swished down with vindictive intent. There was not room for more than three men to ply their swords in the breach at the same time. Finding this sword work did them no good, they withdrew, to prepare for another volley into the room.

This came at last, but it was aimed at random. The candle had been extinguished in the room, and the light of daybreak was still too dim to serve a marksman. The occupants of the room were lying flat against the outer wall, watching the breach, and the bullets hurt no one. They were followed immediately, however, by the desperate invaders. But Rob Roy, being in a position on their flank, was able to stop them. He fired point blank at the nearest man, killing him. The others drew off yet once again.

After that there was peace for a time. The weary garrison lay on the floor until the sun was up. Then Rob Roy and Diarmid rose and looked from the window. Among the shrubs, where the earth had, as they had noticed, been disturbed, was a large hole.

"If we had pried into that matter more carefully we should have discovered their mine in time to prevent this disaster," said Rob Roy.

"Ay, but the turf had been put back so cunningly, and did not give beneath our feet," said Diarmid, "so that no one could have thought the black man had mined a passage from there to the house. He must have been a crafty fellow to work so quietly."

"Some miner from the Lowlands, belike," said Rob Roy. "It must have cost him nights of labour, for he had to carry off the earth when he had dug it out. I wonder he did not begin nearer to the foot of the house."

"He thought we should see the earth had been stirred if he made his opening against the house. Among the bushes it might have escaped our notice, if we had not heard his spade. The sound that wakened us was the barrel of powder rolling against the foundations of the house, I take it."

"Well, they have spared no labour to get at me," said Rob Roy, "but there will be more labour for them yet before they have done."

"I think they have lost enough men and have gone off."

"They will come again. Come, we must mend the breach."

The hole under the breach had been, from the first, filled up with fallen debris. Into the breach Rob Roy and his kinsman now crowded fallen blocks of granite, shattered timbers, heavy furniture, until it was fairly closed by this rough barricade.

Then, posting one of the servants at an upper window to keep watch, they sat down in the wrecked room to eat and drink, keeping loaded muskets and pistols beside them, ready for emergencies.

The morning passed, and nothing happened. Rob Roy and Diarmid fell asleep from sheer exhaustion, and were not awakened until near sunset, when Diarmid started up and called to one of his men.

"The water-jar is empty," he said. "Bring in more water, Dugald." For he was parched with thirst.

"Indeed, sir," said Donald, "there is none in the house, and the rain-barrel is empty."

Diarmid looked grave.

"You must go to the well," he said. Then, taking pity on the old man's evident fears, he added, "Nay, I'll go myself."

He took up an earthen pitcher, and went to the window and climbed out. The well was twenty yards from the house.

Looking about him, Diarmid crossed the open space. He was close to the well when a sharp report sounded, and the pitcher fell in fragments from his hand, shattered by a bullet that had been intended for himself.

The next instant his enemies were running to place themselves between him and the house, in order to cut off his retreat. Three men, standing close against the house, waited, ready to cut him down, while on his left hand, at a little distance from him, a group of men were loading their muskets. He dropped on his knee behind the wall of the well, which sheltered him from this latter peril, and drew a pistol from his belt. The men who intervened between him and the house, luckily for him, had no fire-arms.

With a shrill cry Diarmid called Rob Roy's attention to the strait he was in. The chief appeared at the window.

"I canna get back, Rob Roy," cried Diarmid. "Keep them from stealing round behind me. The well shelters me from their bullets for the present."

So Rob Roy stood with his musket, ready to shoot any man who came within his line of fire, and this kept the enemy from working round to the rear of Diarmid, for the present.

But the rascals in front of him still remained pressed close against the house, where Rob Roy could not easily cover them with his musket.

They were ready to converge upon

Diarmid as soon as he should near the breach, through which he would have to re-enter his house. He had but one pistol, and had not brought his sword with him. He might account for one man, but two would be left to strike at him, an unarmed man for the time being.

Even in that position of deadly peril he could not refrain from trying to get water. He raised his hand to the handle of the windlass, in order to lower the bucket, but instantly withdrew it, and ducked down again, for a bullet whizzed close by his outstretched arm.

At the same moment Rob Roy leaned suddenly from the window, and discharged his musket in a vain attempt to bring down the man who was standing nearest to the breach. The bullet struck the ground in front of him, and he jeered at the Chief's marksmanship. It seemed as if Diarmid was quite cut off from the house and from Rob Roy. To cross the space between the well and the house would be to offer himself as a mark for half a dozen or more muskets, while, if he escaped the bullets, three swords awaited him at the breach.

"They're working round to your rear," shouted Rob Roy, "you must come in, Diarmid."

It was true. Some of the men with muskets were making a wide detour, in order to get among some trees behind him, where they might drive him from the shelter of the wall, and at the same time be out of reach of Rob Roy's bullets. Others remained on the left of the well.

Diarmid, still on one knee, glared defiantly at the three men against the house.

"Can ye hurl my claymore out to me, Rob Roy?" he cried.

The chief nodded, and, by signs, tried to make it clear to Diarmid that he would help him at the breach.

Then he withdrew, to reappear behind the window with Diarmid's bared sword.

One of the enemy crept close under the window. With all his might the Chief threw the claymore. The man under the window sprang up as it passed over his head, and with his blade tried to strike it aside. But it came flashing through the air, hilt foremost, and fell at Diarmid's feet.

He grasped it in his right hand, transferring the pistol to his left. He looked behind him. Four men with fire-arms were creeping within range of him. He sprang up, fired his pistol at one of the men by the house, and then saw Rob Roy emerge from the breach and turn upon one of the others. Diarmid's pistol bullet had failed to take effect, so the next instant he was engaged with two swordsmen. There was a sharp bout of sword play. Rob Roy, however, had sent his opponent running back with a wounded sword-arm, and was able to turn to Diarmid's assistance. Seeing the MacGregors were more than a match for his two men, John Grahame himself dashed towards the house.

But Rob Roy and Diarmid had taken advantage of a momentary retreat of the two pitted against him to dash through the breach, and into the house again.

So they were once more united and behind strong walls, but alas! Diarmid's little expedition had been useless. They were still without water.

CHAPTER IX.

IN DESPERATE PLIGHT.

Disaster now stared them in the face. Men may live in a battered house and succeed in driving off human enemies, so long as they have strength to use weapons of war. But the strongest man cannot hold out very long against that dreadful enemy—thirst. Rob Roy and Diarmid moistened their lips with neat whisky, of which there was still a very little left in the house; but either would have given much for a deep draught of water.

"They'll know our weakness now, and guard the well," said Diarmid. "They've no more need to attack us. If they keep us from the well we're all dead men ere long."

"We must make up our minds to leave the house after dark," said Rob Roy, "and get away down the valley. Since Grahame is here one end of the valley is left open, and we'll return anon with a score of brave laddies and hunt Johnny Grahame over the hills."

It was now nearly dark again, and they began to discuss the possibility of leaving the house. While they were talking there was the crash of a heavy beam against their barricade; some of the rubbish was thrust into the room, an opening appeared, wide enough to admit one man, and there was one man in the opening.

Rob Roy ran at him, with the sword he chanced to be nursing when the crash came, and the man disappeared. But the weary MacGregors knew that all chance of stealing away was gone, and that they were in for another night of vigil and fighting. Grahame, angered by the wound he had incurred in his previous encounter with Rob Roy, was more determined to make good the boast he had uttered to Campbell of Ruthin and George Murray than he had been when he made it.

That night was much as the previous night had been. There were intervals of complete silence, lasting sometimes for more than an hour, and then a spirt of flame would flash through the breach and a report fill the room, or a man would suddenly strive desperately to get in ; but always with the same result. The would-be invader always retired precipitately before the gleam of Rob Roy's sword. A candle had been lighted to illumine the breach, so that no one could steal in under cover of darkness. Now and then, by way of variety, a bullet whistled through the unglazed window ; but no harm was done by these missiles, except to Diarmid's kitchen wall, for the occupants of the room remained flat upon the floor, with eyes fixed upon the breach, and now and then upon the window.

Parched lips had been wetted with the last drop of whisky, and despair seized upon Diarmid. They must have water soon, or die.

At midnight a beam crashed against the barricade again, and the opening was made a little wider.

Diarmid rose, and leaning out of the window, fired at the men who carried this battering-ram. He wounded one of them, and they dropped the beam and went round the corner of the house.

" We've harmed them more than they have harmed us," said Diarmid, with savage satisfaction. " When we've hit them all we can get to the well."

This was his only hope now, to put all his enemies out of the fight. It was a shadowy hope. They were numerous, and although many had been wounded, there were more who had not been touched. But Diarmid, growing desperate with thirst, remained boldly at the window, with three loaded muskets beside him, ready to fire whenever he had a chance of aiming at anyone.

Before the sun rose he had fired all three muskets, with what success he did not know ; after firing the third, at something which may have been a man, he went to the table, which had been put on its legs again after having been inverted by the explosion, to get another charge for his muskets.

" The powder's gone ! " he said aghast.

" I've one charge left in my pistol," said Rob Roy.

" Then we're all dead men. We cannot harm them now, for what use are swords against muskets ? "

He leaned on his musket, pale, red-eyed from want of sleep, and stared hopelessly at his Chief.

" We're in a bad case, Diarmid, and that's the truth," said Rob Roy. " If it were not for your honest fellows I would propose that we should draw our swords and go out, and trust to Providence and cold steel to carry us safely through the ring of our enemies. But your men are too old for such rough work as that."

" Ay, 'tis true," said Diarmid.

" I would go alone," said Rob Roy, " if I thought it would draw these men away from your house ; as I have brought trouble upon you by being here I would run any risk to draw it away from you. But, were I dead, or safely away, I fear they would not leave you. They have seen your walls splashed with the blood of their friends, and they will avenge it if they can."

" Ay, they will do that."

" We must hope that the noise of this siege has spread abroad by now. How far off is your nearest neighbour ? "

" Eight good miles, and he is no great friend of mine, to tell the truth, though he would, perhaps, no care to know there were strangers in the valley. Then there is the little buddel, but that is nine miles to the south, and not many travellers pass that way. If help does not come to-day I shall die of thirst, or go daft."

The probability of help coming from outside, in that thinly-populated district, was very remote. Here were five men shut up in a battered house, without water, and prowling about the house were an unascertained number of fierce, well-armed men. The odds against Rob Roy were very heavy.

Day broadened, and the enemy remained out of sight. Then they came, ten of them, rushing towards the breach, and Rob Roy and Diarmid crouched on the floor again. As usual, bullets came first, then swordsmen. Rob Roy cut at the first man who retired, cut at the second, who also retired ; no one followed these two.

"They're out of powder," roared Grahame. Diarmid groaned. The enemy knew all their weak places now.

After that Grahame's ruffians showed themselves, at first timorously, then more boldly, in front of the window, and in close proximity to the house. They jeered at the MacGregors, and laughed mockingly ; then some of them got to work at the well, pulling up water. Diarmid, leaning against the window frame, saw them raising the bucket to their lips, and his sufferings were intensified ; again he groaned dolefully.

"Now, my brave fellows," shouted Grahame at last, "they've no more powder, so we may go in and finish them. Ye need not be afraid to use the beam."

He called to several of the men to pick it up. One ruffian, being unoccupied, strolled carelessly up to the window.

"Would you like any powder in there ? " he asked, tauntingly, standing just under the window.

Rob Roy rose silently, and appeared suddenly at the window. "I've all I need," he said, grimly, and so fired his last charge, and shot the fellow through the head.

The men with the battering-ram, seeing this, wavered ; then they dropped the beam and fled before Rob Roy's empty pistol ; but Grahame sent a pistol bullet singing close past Rob Roy's head, and the Chief, with a careless laugh, withdrew from his perilous position.

After that there was a respite from fighting—though none from the torments of thirst and sleeplessness. At noon there was the sound of a pibroch, echoing down the valley, and sudden hope flushed Diarmid's face, until he recognised the pipe of the Campbells. They might be friendly Campbells, though that was improbable. Between hope and fear he stood where he could spy out of the windows, until Campbell of

Ruthin came strutting into view, with a piper and a dozen men, and then hope died out utterly. The enemy was reinforced. The Campbells, no less than Grahame, had good cause to wish Rob Roy and all his companions dead, or they would incur not only the wrath of the MacGregors for their late attempts upon Rob Roy's life, but also, possibly, the stern displeasure of their lawful head, the great Duke of Argyll. The lips that could speak to their late doings must be silenced for ever if Campbell of Ruthin was to live in comfort.

Grahame and Campbell met in front of the house.

"What, Campbell, man," said the former, "have you brought your siller bullet ? "

"Losh, man, is the red thief yet alive ? I see you've made a hole in the house. Why dinna ye go in and finish your work ? "

"There's little need for that. Time will finish them. But maybe ye're parched after your march. A draught of cool well-water will refresh ye."

He led Campbell off to the well, talking as he went. Presently the Campbells got hold of the beam, and charged with a will at the barricade. Alas ! there were no bullets to stop them. The barricade tottered, fell in with a crash, and there was a space again where three men could enter abreast.

Three did enter, but only two got out. A short clatter of swords, and there was only a fallen man in the breach. He was pulled away presently.

This filled Campbell with rage.

"If they've no more powder, they are in our hands," he shouted. "To the breach, lads, some of ye, and some to the window. I'll show you the way."

A few seconds later he had leapt valorously in at the window, to be spitted at once on Rob Roy's sword. Diarmid, at the breach, was assisted by one of his men. Rob Roy lifted Campbell's body, and flung it down upon others who were trying to get in at the window.

"Campbell's dead, Campbell's dead ! " The cry rose, shrill and sudden. The men storming the breach drew back aghast. There was confusion and uproar outside. The dead Campbell was carried away, and the whole band withdrew out of view.

"The next assault will be the worst

we've had to deal with yet," said Rob Roy.

" Oh ! man, I'd give all I have for a draught from the well," said Diarmid.

" I would do the same," said Rob Roy.

One of the servants was lying in a corner, moaning pitifully for want of water. The situation was at last plainly hopeless.

" We cannot leave the old men, or we could get away yet by the back door," said Rob Roy.

" We could not travel far, even then, without being seen and overtaken."

" No. Well, Diarmid, here's farewell to ye ; and I take shame to myself to think I've brought this trouble upon you." He gave the young man his hand.

" Losh ! man, 'tis nothing. To die fighting beside my Chief is a right good Highland death, and I do not heed it at all. Hush ! here they come."

Rob Roy sprang to the breach, Diarmid to the window.

The men came on, Grahame's men and the Campbells, fierce, vindictive, and determined. A volley crashed and bullets sped through the room. Then there were swords twinkling in the breach, and Rob Roy was beating them aside, parrying, cutting, thrusting for his life. Swords were leaping about the window, and Diarmid was stabbing down at the men who clustered beneath him. Other men were trying to batter in the door. If that went, the game was up. Two men could not guard three places of entry ; the servants were no swordsmen, and one of them was all but helpless.

The attackers drew back, fierce as ever, but a little winded by their efforts. They had not forced an entrance yet.

But two weary men could scarcely make another effort, and crashing blows were still being dealt at the door.

CHAPTER X.

THE SWINGING HALTER.

The door withstood the blows that were dealt upon it so well that the men desisted for awhile from their task, and joined the others who were grouped about Grahame, near the well.

Deliberately they refreshed themselves with water, in full view of the parched men in the house, and then as deliberately reloaded muskets and pistols. Grahame was plainly giving orders in preparation for the next assault upon the house.

The men marshalled in three parties. One party had got hold of a heavy beam, with which to drive a tilt at the door. It could not withstand that sort of assault very long.

The second party, armed with swords, cast glances towards the window ; their mission was easy to guess. The third party handled muskets.

Grahame addressed them all vigorously in Gaelic. Then he gave the word for the attack.

" They're coming now, chief."

" Ay, I'll take the musketeers in the flank when they're through the breach. I can cut down one or two."

" I could guard the windows for awhile, but it's the door—it's the door where they'll have us. It'll never hold. Here they come."

The three parties ran forward. There was a heavy thud as the end of the beam struck the house door, which had not yielded yet. Then two men got into the breach and tried to aim their muskets at a living mark ; but Rob Roy, close against the wall, on their left hand, kept out of their line of fire and at the same time cut at their fingers, until one of them, forced into the room by the pressure of eager comrades behind him, fell a victim to the chief's sword.

But others pressed forward ; amid the musket barrels Rob Roy strove desperately ; Diarmid was keeping down the men who would have climbed through the window, but one of them called out, " Come and shoot this fellow, one of you." A musketeer left the breach and came towards the window. At the same time the door crashed beneath the second blow of the battering-ram. The men would be through it in a minute.

All seemed to be at an end.

But sudden and shrill there rose once more the sound of a pibroch. It was not the Campbell's piper that was playing. And then, their kilts swinging, their claymores flashing, a score of stalwart MacGregors came racing across the valley. The attackers did not notice them at first, but Diarmid saw them.

He raised the war-cry of Clan Gregor, and loud and fierce was the response. The wild cry echoed down the valley. Grahame heard it at last, turned, and saw what threatened him. The Campbells were off and away ; but Grahame's men left the breach, and threw down the beam, only just in time to defend themselves. The MacGregors, with a whoop, were in amongst them, plying their swords with exultant glee; and Rob Roy ran out, to be hailed with a glad cry of triumphant welcome, and joined in the fray.

The claymores of Clan Gregor soon cleared the ground of enemies—except, indeed, of dead ones—and the clansmen leaned on their swords, and wondered at the story which Diarmid and the chief had to tell them, after they had quenched their thirst at the well.

That night there was feasting and laughter in Diarmid's battered house. The next day, and for some days after, the MacGregors remained at the house, busily repairing the damage that had been done to it, until no traces were left of the recent remarkable attack upon it.

Now that Rob Roy had a strong escort about him, Grahame and Murray no longer tarried in the neighbourhood of the valley, where, indeed, they would no longer have been safe in any case; for all the people for miles round had heard of their misdeeds, and were on the look-out for them.

So the boast that three men had made in the lonely inn proved to be a vain one, and Campbell of Ruthin had lost his life in trying to make it good.

Satisfied that Diarmid would have no more trouble from his enemies, Rob Roy at last took leave of him, and led his armed band miles and miles away over the hills, to his lofty mountain cave, the Eagles' Nest.

During all this time the chief had not forgotten the remarkable signs that had been painted on the lonely cairn to warn him of danger, and he puzzled much over them. Diarmid was more than ever assured, after the attack upon his house, that the fairies had been responsible for them. What human ally could have had foreknowledge of Grahame's gunpowder plot? A human friend, even if he could have had any such knowledge, would surely have come to the house to give verbal warning.

Rob Roy was to arrive at a solution of the mystery unexpectedly, when the matter had nearly passed from his mind.

One bleak winter's day he set out, with two of his men, to carry some money to a clansman who dwelt about halfway between the Eagles' Nest and Diarmid's house, and who was being pressed for rent by a harsh landlord.

The hills were white with snow, and they would have to make a long march if they did not wish to camp out in the open at night—no very attractive prospect at that inclement season of the year.

The winter twilight comes early in Scotland, and the dark began to gather when their journey was but half accomplished. The snow had obliterated all tracks, and a thick veil of snow clouds hid the stars. Consequently Rob Roy and his companions, although so well-accustomed to wandering among the mountains at all seasons of the year, lost their way after the dark had fairly set in.

This dilemma was not so alarming to Highlanders as it might have been to some folks. They carried food and whisky with them, and their plaids would serve, at a shift, for bedding, if they could shelter in the lee of some rock. But they had no wish to pass the night in the open unless absolutely obliged to do so.

They wandered on through the darkness until a late hour, when Rob Roy said, "I cannot judge which way we are going, and as we may be travelling away from our destination I think we must make a halt."

"We are going right, if the wind is any guide," said one of the men, "but it may have shifted a point or two."

"Ay," replied the chief, "indeed, I think we had better halt until the clouds break and show us the stars."

It was a cheerless prospect, but they made towards some snow-covered rocks, intending to rest for some hours, at all events, when one of the men said gleefully, "See, there's a fire yonder."

They raised their eyes, and saw a twinkling point of fire on a mountain spur in front of them.

"Who would camp out in this season?" said Rob Roy, "except gipsies? Well, the gipsies have ever been good friends of mine. We will join them awhile, and perhaps, when we have warmed ourselves at their fire they will be able to put us on our right path."

Accordingly they tramped through the snow towards the fire. As they drew nearer to it they saw that there were many people gathered about it. The camping place had been well-chosen. It was sheltered from the wind by lofty rocks, and was, indeed, girdled round by rocks, while a few storm-twisted trees grew on the spot.

"They must certainly be gipsies," said Rob Roy, "unless they be broken men, like the robbers we drove out of Glen Ramond. Keep your swords handy lads; though I hope they are gipsies, when there is sure to be a pot boiling and a cheery welcome awaiting us."

The suspicion that these might be roving thieves, who camped on the hills, because they dared not venture near inhabited places, caused the MacGregors to steal up towards the fire cautiously.

The men gathered about the fire could not see much beyond the circle of light it cast, so Rob Roy and his two companions drew close up to them unobserved. Then, with an exclamation of anger, Rob Roy dropped down behind a rock; his companions did the same, and they could see without being seen. It was a strange sight that met their eyes—an ominous sight. A dozen kilted men were gathered on one side of the fire. Opposite them stood a young man, his hands tied behind him, and from one of the twisted trees near by hung a length of rope with a noose at the end of it. It was swinging gently to and fro in the cold night wind.

Rob Roy's followers could make nothing of this strange scene; but the chief had his eyes fixed upon the central figure of the group about the fire.

John Grahame and Geordie Murray sat side by side, and when rogues put their heads together there is sure to be trouble brewing for honest men.

CHAPTER XI.

A TIMELY RESCUE.

The young man, who was bound, stood with his back turned towards Rob Roy, who could make no guess as to his identity, but who saw that he was being tried before this rough tribunal, which consisted of a nondescript collection of rogues in the pay of Grahame and Murray.

"You heard all we said at the buddel, did ye not?" said Grahame to the prisoner.

"I gave it no thought," said the latter; "ye were mostly fou, ye ken."

Grahame frowned. "Was it for you to notice if a gentleman was fou or sober? Well, if our tongues wagged

faster than they should you learned all the more, and were, therefore, the more easily able to do us this mischief."

"I did ye no mischief. I filled your glasses when you called to me. I'm a poor, harmless body—indeed, and that's the truth."

"You're no so simple as you would have folks believe. You learnt all our plans for trapping the fox, and, by the same token, I charge ye, therefore, with the death of Campbell o' Ruthin. You warned Rob Roy of what was coming."

"I've na spoken with the great MacGregor these many months; since he paid my mother's rent, but for which she would have been turned out, sick as she was, in the snow."

"You see, he has a reason for befriending the MacGregor," said Murray.

"Ay, and cannily he contrived it."

"I never spoke to him," persisted the prisoner.

"Ye were seen carrying a pot of paint, and there were signs painted, on a place no doubt selected by Rob Roy, to bid him which way to turn to avoid danger," said Murray.

"Rob Roy has many friends," pleaded the prisoner.

"And you are one of them."

"Indeed, ay. Poor Davy is a friend to all you braw fighting men. He has filled all your glasses many a time."

"But will do so no more, I think. You should have kept to the liquor shop, my lad, and not gone astraying on the hills."

"My master never made any complaint of me."

"Your master is drunk and abed most times."

"Enough," said Grahame, savagely, "the fellow whom we thought a simpleton, was a spy in the pay of MacGregor. That's plain enough. He slipped out between whiles to converse with Rob Roy by means of signs, which was the reason why the MacGregor was able to send word to his clansmen to come and get him out of the trap we had him in. Hang him, hang him! Bear a hand there, Robin, Sandy, any of you. Lead him to the tree, and hoist him up. No man, daft or sane, shall cross John Grahame."

Rob Roy had listened to all this with amazement. The mystery of the cairn was solved at last. Daft Davy, from the lonely drinking-shop, heard much talk during the performance of his duties. He had thus learnt all about the traps laid for the chief of the MacGregors, and in return for a kindly act performed by the latter had tried to save him from danger. His spare time was brief, but he had contrived to get out, now and again, as far as to the lonely cairn. Possibly he could never spare the time to travel so far as Diarmid's house, perhaps he feared to be seen near it. He must have known the cairn to be Rob Roy's look-out post, and, because he could not write, or employ a messenger, he had invented a language of his own, a language of pictures, trusting that the chief would have sufficient perspicacity to understand it.

Well, Rob Roy had at last come to understand it ; he marvelled at the simple lad's devotion and ingenuity. The poor fellow had risked much upon the bare chance of being able to serve him, and now he was to be hanged for his service.

The men about the fire were all of one mind. Daft Davy was too clever by half to be suffered to live amongst them any more.

" Ye'll spare my life, John Grahame, ye'll spare my life, Mr. Murray," said the lad shrilly. " I've a widowed mother, Mr. Murray."

Murray shook his head and turned away.

Davy was by now in the hands of two ruffianly fellows, and he thought that his case was hopeless.

" Very well," he said, to Grahame and Murray, " maybe I did paint up pictures that might speak to Rob Roy, whiles and again, to warn him against three black villains that plotted to kill him. And I hope ye may both come within reach of his sword. It's little stand you'd make against him,

when a score of you could not touch him, ye poor feckless bodies."

Then, without a struggle, he suffered himself to be led to the fatal tree.

Rob Roy had already drawn his sword.

" Up, lads, let them hear the slogan of Clan Gregor," he whispered to his wondering comrades.

With a shrill yell, that might have proceeded from a dozen lusty throats, the three MacGregors leapt over the rocks, with swords uplifted, into the circle of firelight.

Half the men scrambled up hastily, and scattered back.

Grahame rose, but almost before he could draw his sword Rob Roy was upon him. He managed to evade the first blow, and bare his claymore.

Then, in the firelight, a terrific combat commenced. While Rob Roy and Grahame did battle together one of the MacGregors singled out Murray, and drove him back and back into the darkness, until his sword broke, and he ran for his life. The other MacGregors had an easy task of it in dispersing those of the men who had not already run away, for they had been surprised so suddenly that they had no time to get their arms, which were lying by the fire.

After a sharp contest Grahame threw up his arms and fell. He had come within reach of Rob Roy's sword sooner than Davy could have hoped, and would compass murder and other dark deeds no more.

In a few minutes not a man of the band remained visible.

Davy's bonds were cut, and Rob Roy, aware at last who was the mysterious friend who had warned him so oddly when beset by dangers, took him into his own service, where he was safe from the vengeance of lawless men.

THE END.

Published by JAMES HENDERSON & SONS, at Red Lion House, Red Lion-court, Fleet-street, E.C

www.ingramcontent.com/pod-product-compliance
Lightning Source LLC
Chambersburg PA
CBHW082053220626
47052CB00006B/1229